LONE WOMAN OF GHALAS-HAT

By
Rice D. Oliver

Dedicated To:
Bonnie, Jacob, Christa and Cynthia

Published & Distributed by
California Weekly Explorer, Inc.
285 E. Main St., Suite 3
Tustin, CA 92780
(714) 730-5991
ISBN 0-936778-51-2 Paper Cover
ISBN 0-936778-52-0 Hard Cover

Cover and Illustrations by Charles Zafuto

©**Copyright 1999, 1993 by California Weekly Explorer, Inc.** Tustin, California 92780. This book and all contents are fully protected by the copyright laws of the United States. Reproduction by any process for any purpose is prohibited without the express written permission of the publisher. Infringement of copyright is subject to prosecution and violators are subject to both civil and criminal liability.

Manufactured in the United States of America

Far from the shores of Ventura County in California is the island of San Nicolas. The Indians called it *Ghalas-hat.* It is 70 miles from the coast. It is the last land off the coast, a lonely place where the winds blow hard and only the sound of birds and seals and the crashing of the waves is heard. The seals, sea lions, sea elephants and birds like this loneliness. It means that they can be safe from the harm of people. Large groups of them have made their home on the beaches of the island.

For hundreds of years the people of *Ghalashat* lived on the island. They had learned to make homes from brush and driftwood. They knew where to find the bird eggs and how to kill a few animals for food and clothing. The playful sea otter lived in large numbers in the sea around the island. The sea otter lived on the abalone shellfish it pried from the rocks. It could be seen by the Indians as it floated along on its back pounding the shellfish on a small rock it carried on its tummy. It would pound the shell until the meat broke loose and then enjoy a delicious

meal. The Indians ate the abalone too, but they did not mind sharing it with the sea otters. The sea otter had warm fur the Indians could use for clothing whenever they killed one. After many years of living on the island, the Indians had learned to live with the resources of the island.

The Indians built boats and traded with Indians on Santa Catalina Island many miles away. They made their boats from the driftwood much the same way as the Chumash did. Sometimes they made boats from the logs that drifted ashore too.

All of this changed. The Russians came with their Aleut friends from Alaska. They came to kill the otter for its fur. They killed the seals too. They did not want enough fur for their own clothes. They wanted all of the fur. They did not care if the Indians needed the otter and seals too. They wanted to sell the fur to people in Russia and Asia. When the Indians were in the way, they killed them too. The Americans came from Boston. They brought Kodiak Indians and left them on the island to take whatever otter and seal fur was left. More Indians were killed. Soon there were only about 25 Indian people of *Ghalas-hat* left on the island.

The padres of Santa Barbara Mission called the island San Nicolas and the people were called the Nicoleños. They seemed to be the only ones who cared about the few people left. They asked an American sea captain to take his boat to the island and bring the people to the mainland for safety. In 1835 the ship came to the island for the people. When it arrived, a great storm came. The winds blew so hard that the ship was in danger of being sent upon the rocks. The captain quickly had the people of *Ghalas-hat* pack their things and get on the ship. "We must sail now, or we will be cast upon

the rocks and our ship will sink. Hurry, hurry," he urged. The people hurried aboard the ship.

"Wait! Where is my baby?" one young mother called. She thought it had been brought aboard the ship by another person. She could not find it on the ship. She became upset. "It must still be on the island! We must go get it!" she pleaded with the captain.

"We cannot go back now," he said. "The ship will be wrecked, and we could all be killed!" He promised they would sail away from the island and would come back the next day and search for the baby.

The young mother looked at the island. She knew the great dangers that were there for her child. The storm could blow the hut in on the baby. The wild dogs could harm it. There was no one to hold it when it was crying. Who would feed it? She saw that the ship was leaving the island. She must get to her baby now.

The waves had become very large. The wind was blowing hard. The island was getting farther away. "I must go to my baby!" she called, and she threw herself into the ocean. The huge waves tossed her about and she had trouble keeping her head above the water. She began to swim, and swim, and swim. Her arms ached. She swallowed great gulps of salty water.

The people on the ship looked at her small body in the water. They could see her head among the waves. "She will never make it. Not even a strong sailor can swim in that kind of sea," they said. The captain promised he would come back and look for her. He sailed for San Pedro with the rest of the Indians.

The young mother finally made it to the beach. She had been tossed about by the waves. Her body ached, but she had made it to the shore. She was too tired and sore to stand, but she forced herself to her feet. She hurried to the place where she last saw the child. There was no sign of it. She searched the beaches and the canyons. She looked everyplace. After many hours of looking, she knew the baby would never be found alive.

She fell to her knees and started to sob. Her tired muscles gave up, and she lay back in the tall grass and shut her eyes. For many hours she thought about her baby and what could have happened to it. She started to cry and cry. She cried until there were no more tears. Then she thought about herself. The ship was gone. Would it come back for her? Would she be alone here forever?

"Maybe they will come for me when the storm stops," she thought. There was not another person left on the island. The Russians were gone, the Aleuts had left, the Kodiaks were gone, and now all of her people were gone. She had come back for her child, but it was gone too! Now there were only the birds, and seals and wild dogs and the young mother left on San Nicolas Island. She had become the Lone Woman of Ghalas-hat.

The storm stopped the next day. She watched for a sail. None ever came. After many days she gave up hope of being taken away from the lonely island. She knew now that she would have to remember everything she had learned as a child. If she was to have a home, she would have to make it for herself. If she was hungry, she would have to hunt for food. She would have to fish, catch crabs or shellfish, dig roots, find water. If she wanted warm clothes, she would have to make them from the bird skins or furs. If she wanted a fire, she would have to start one herself, without matches.

Her love for her child had brought her to the island again when all of her friends were leaving. Now she would have to meet a very hard test to see if she should take care of herself on a lonely island. Would she pass the test?

The captain of the ship had planned to return to San Nicolas Island to see if the young mother had made it safely to the island and to bring her to Santa Barbara Mission. He never did. He had been sent to San Francisco and his ship turned over as it entered the bay. The ship was lost. Now there wasn't another

large ship on all of the coast of Southern California. No one wanted to make the dangerous trip in the small Chumash boats. Most people thought she had drowned, that if the young mother had made it to shore, she was alone and without any real hope of being saved.

The young mother knew the island well. It had always been her home. She could remember all of the places where fresh water could be found. She knew the best rocks to search along the shore for abalone and other food from the tidepools. She had learned which plants were good for food. She knew how to make a hut from the things she found on the island. Before all of her people left, they had shared some of these jobs. She knew now that she would have to do them all herself.

One of the first things she had to do was the hardest. She would have to make a fire to keep warm on the cold foggy nights and to cook her food. This was something she had not done before. The fires had always been kept burning. There were no matches on Ghalas-hat. Keeping the fires going was important. At night it could be cold on the island. Fires kept the wild dogs away from camp too. The dogs had been left on the island by ships and had become wild and mean.

When a fire wasn't needed, the Indians covered it with ashes. This kept the burnt wood hot. When a fire was needed, the ashes were removed and dry grass was added to the glowing embers. By blowing on the embers, the Indians could get the fire to come up again. When the Indians had left the island, all of the fires went out. The young mother had watched some of the older Indians start fires a few times. She took some dry grass and placed it below a flat stick. Using a sharp shell, she carefully made a groove in the stick. Then she put some of the grass close to the groove. She found a long pointed stick and rubbed it in the groove. It took a

long time. She rubbed hard. She felt the end of the stick. It was warm. She rubbed harder. The stick was turning dark from the heat. There was still no fire. Harder and harder and faster and faster she rubbed the stick. She saw some smoke. She blew on the smoke. Again she rubbed the sticks. Her arm muscles were getting sore. She kept rubbing. More smoke came. The grass started to smoke now. She picked it up carefully and blew on it. She became excited when she saw the glow of the embers. She added some dry sticks. Again she blew. The fire burst into flames. "Ahhhheee!" she yelled. She had a fire. She knew she must keep it going. This became one of her most important jobs.

When the night came, the fire would keep her warm. It would help her cook her food. It would keep away the wild dogs. She would be able to use it for light. The fire would help dry her on wet nights. She always gathered wood for her fire. She covered the ashes to keep them warm when she left her camp. She carefully uncovered them when she returned. She would add grass and dry wood to the ashes for another fire. When she traveled the island, she took ashes with her in an abalone shell. After many weeks of wandering the island, she had fires carefully hidden in many places. She was always careful to keep the fire away from dry grass. She did not want a fire to burn up all of her firewood or her food.

The young mother built a new hut. She found some long sticks that had washed up on the shore. She dug small holes in a circle. She put a long stick in each hole and tied them together at the top. She took brush and piled it against the sides of the sticks. She buried the outside edge of her hut in sand. She had thought about the cruel people who had killed so many of her friends. What if they came back for more sea otters? She decided to make her huts low and in secret places where she could see the beaches if they came ashore.

One day she saw a strange thing down on the beach. She couldn't tell what it was from her hillside hut. She ran to the beach and found some whale ribs. She often watched the huge whales swimming by her island. She remembered once when some had made a mistake and turned as they swam. They came right up on the beach. Her people had killed some of them and had much food for many months. They used the bones for tools and many things.

"These bones will be useful to me," she thought. She dragged them to a new place she had thought of for making a home. She arranged them to make the side of her hut. She wove some mats from the grass. It was a fine home. She was close to one of the places she gathered food. Fresh water was near too.

One day she thought about her clothes. Some of the nights are very cold on Ghalas-hat. "The seabirds seem to be warm even on the coldest days. They have a fine coat of feathers." She thought about it for a while. Then she started to plan. Whenever she trapped a bird or found one dead on the sand, she carefully removed its skin with its feathers. She dried the skin in the warm sunlight. After she had enough skins, she carefully sewed them together. She used pieces of bone for a needle. She used some of the hard parts of the muscles of birds for thread. She was very careful to sew the dress so the seams were hidden. Finally she had a fine dress of blue, green, and black feathers. She admired her dress and enjoyed its warmth.

On some days the storms came in across the Pacific Ocean and made even her best hut a cold and wet place. The wind blew very hard. These days were the ones that reminded her of how very alone she was. She remembered that day many years before when she last saw anyone. She had never even spoken to a person for many years. She thought about this and made a new plan. She would

make a huge pile of brush near one of her camps. Then she would watch for a ship. The first time she saw one, she would light the brush. The people on the ship would see the fire and smoke and come and take her to her people.

One day when she was watching the ocean, she saw a ship. It was getting closer. She ran to her fire. She thought how it would be to be able to talk to her people again. Then she thought again, "What if that ship is full of the ones who killed so many of my people? They will surely kill me too." She didn't light her signal fire. She watched the ship as it went by very close. She hid low in the grass. It sailed by and was gone. Then she thought again, "But, it could have been the ship of the people who would take me away to my own people!" She began to cry. "Would she ever see people again?" She lay in the sand looking at the clouds above for a very long time. She thought about the many years she had been alone. It had been ten years now since she had spoken to anyone. She was about 18 years old when she first came back to the island looking for her baby. In all of that time she had never spoken to another person. She had never had any help from anyone. She had found and cooked her own food. She had made her own clothes. She built her own homes. She had found secret places all over the island. She had moved her main living place to a cave on one end of the island. She knew good places to store food where the wild animals would never find it. She was a person who could take care of herself, but she wanted to see people.

She had made some friends among the island animals. The dogs were too wild to come near. But one day she found some pups whose mother had died. They were still playful and friendly. She fed them and they began to follow her. They were her friends for many years on the island.

She had thought about what would happen if she got injured or sick or too old to hunt. She made a plan. She would hide food close to her many camps and always close to the few places where fresh water could be found. If she was too ill to travel, she would be able to crawl to each place. The many days she spent planning and making things she needed helped her in her loneliness. She talked to the dogs. She spoke of the things she knew: the sky, the sea, the sea otter, the wind, the birds. She told the dogs of her sadness at being alone. She told them about the happy days when she had her own child. She told them about the people who lived on the island many years before. They didn't really know what she was saying, but it helped to have someone to listen anyway.

One day she was resting in her whalebone hut. It was one of her favorite places. She was watching the clouds above. Suddenly, she heard voices of men. She jumped up and peeked around the sand dune. There were men on the beach below. They were dragging a boat ashore. The sudden sound of voices had startled her. "I must hide!" she thought. She began to crawl through the sand until she got far enough away that she knew they would not see her. Then she got to her feet and ran. Her dogs ran toward the men on the beach growling and barking.

The men looked up at the dogs running toward them. They picked up rocks and hit one of the dogs. These pet dogs had always been treated kindly by the woman, but the men thought they were some of the wild dogs. The dogs yelped and ran after the Indian woman.

She had spent all of her life on this island. It was her whole world, and she knew every cave and canyon from one end of it to the other. She vanished as easily as footprints washed by the waves. Able to blend quickly with the sand and brush, she was soon safe from the searchers.

The men had come to the beach to search for furs and to fish. But they were not the cruel ones who had come many years before. They had heard the story of the woman and decided to search for her too. It had been 15 years now since she was left there, and Padre Gonzales had sent Thomas Jeffries to the island to look for the woman. He searched the island, and he found one of the huts. But it did not look like anyone had used it for many years. "If she ever was here, she is probably dead now," he told his men. They returned to Santa Barbara with the news that no one was on the island. He told the people the island was 7 or 8 miles long and about 3 miles wide. He told them about the interesting hut made of whale bones. He showed them a cup he found. He also told them about the many otters that were once again at San Nicolas Island. For many weeks the lost woman of San Nicolas was talked about at Santa Barbara. Was she there? Could anyone live that long alone on an island? What about the hut and the cup?

An American seaman, Captain George Nidiver, heard these many stories. He wanted to find out if the woman could still be on the island. He wanted to find some of these sea otters too. He hired a crew of Indians and took his ship to the island. They landed on the beach on a sunny day when the butterflies

were there. The cactus were covered with yellow flowers. There was no sign of any human life. They looked around for a short time for the woman, and then they saw the seals and the sea otters. They lost interest in the search. They killed seals and sea otters. They made a camp on the beach using oars and a piece of sail for a tent. They stayed there 6 weeks.

They caught the seal when it slept on the beach. The seals were not used to people and were not afraid as the men sneaked up on them with ropes. Within a few minutes a seal could be caught, killed and skinned. The sea otters were caught by throwing nets into the sea where they played in large numbers. When it was very windy, the sea otter would bury its head under the kelp and would not see the man coming with their nets.

The men stayed until they had all of the furs they could carry in their boat. They took down their tent and rowed their small boat to the ship. The woman had been watching them and had been thinking about going to them. How she would like to talk to people again. But she could not know for sure if they would be kind or cruel. She knew some of them were Indians, but she didn't understand their words. And she had not understood the words of the cruel men who killed her people.

As the men got into the ship and made ready to leave, a big wind came. The seas were boiling with waves. The mast broke on the ship. The anchor chain broke. The men had to work hard to save the ship. They fixed it and started sailing away in the rough sea, hoping to get away from the dangers of being washed onto the rocks.

One of the men looked at the island through the rough spray of the sea. "What a lonely place to spend even a few weeks. I don't think any woman ever lived there for years," he said. Just then he saw a figure of a person on the hill.
He blinked his eyes and leaned over the rail to see better. "Look, look,

it's her!" he yelled through the storm. The others looked at the hill as the spray got heavier. Soon the figure was gone.

"It must have been a tree," one said, "No, no, she was running along the hill waving at us like she wanted us to see her," he replied. But once again the ship had to leave and make for safer places.

When the ship returned to Santa Barbara they told the people of the strange sight. In July, 1853, 18 years after the woman had first been left alone on the island, Captain Nidiver once again sailed for San Nicolas. He was going to search the island until he proved one way or another that the woman was alive or dead or never on the island. He knew there were old huts and signs that people had been on the island. These could be hers or they could have been left by fishermen. He must have something better to prove if she is there or not.

The first night they landed on the island and set up their camp. Captain Nidiver walked along the beach with Charles Brown, a friend. He looked at the waves washing in on the lonely sand. Then, suddenly, he stopped. "Look! There in the sand! A footprint!" It was a slender small footprint. And a whole trail of them led away from the beach to the low sand hills. "It's her. It has to be. She is living. After all of these years she still lives," he yelled.

"**W**e are friends," he called. "We have come to take you to your people. Come out to us. We won't hurt you." He knew the woman must be very near. The waves had not even washed away her footprints yet. He felt very sad that he had been here before and not found her. "How lonely she must have been and how afraid of us not to come out." He thought of how she had been seen running along the hills waving at them.

They searched and searched for her. They found some of her hidden food. They found a new dress she had started to make out of bird feathers. They found her camps. But they did not find her. "She must know every cave and hiding place on this island," he said to his friend. "We will get the crew

and start searching this island, and we are not leaving until we find her."

They searched for days. No one could find her. They began to think that the footprints must have been something else. The moonlight may have fooled them. But Captain Nidiver wanted to search one more time before leaving. Again they searched. Captain Nidiver found a piece of driftwood a long distance away from the beach. "Someone carried it here," he said. "She is here and we will find her."

"We are looking for a ghost," the other men said. "If she was ever here, she is gone now. We have looked everywhere. Let's go back to our families." But they knew the captain had made up his mind and they searched again.

Charles Brown climbed to the highest hill. He looked around the island in every direction. He could see the men searching along the shore and the hills. Then he saw what looked like a crow in the bushes. He crawled along toward the object. "A bird would see me by now and fly away," he thought. As he got closer, he saw that it was the head of the Indian woman. She was hiding in one of her huts watching the men below and had not seen him coming. He stopped and watched her. He saw that she had a knife. He saw a small fire burning nearby. He heard her talking to herself. It must have been her own voice that kept her from hearing him.

As he walked toward her, he spoke. She quickly turned around. Her dogs growled and showed their teeth. She was surprised, but she called to the dogs and they became quiet. Suddenly she smiled. It was over. Finally a person had found her. She would be able to speak to someone. She could once again see her people.

The Indian woman wanted the man to know she was friendly. She gave him some food. He smiled and took it. He called to the others and they came. They did not understand what she said, but they knew she was happy to see them and to talk. They all tasted her food. They made motions to her to pack her things and follow them to the beach. She understood and took her favorite things. All of them she had made. She left her dogs. They had been her only friends on the island these 18 years. But they would be happier here with their own and in their own home. She knew what it was like to be away from your own people.

The Indian woman went with the men to Santa Barbara. She told the people there of her life on the island. They did not understand her words. They sent for her people to explain her words. Not one of her people, the people of Ghalas-hat, could be found. Many had died. Others had mixed with other Indians and were no longer a people together.

There were many sights at Santa Barbara that were exciting to the Indian woman. She had never seen a horse or a wagon or large homes. She had never seen so many people. She had never heard the church bells ring or the music of the singers. She enjoyed the sights and sounds. She lived with Captain Nidiver and his wife. People came and visited and brought gifts. She always saved the gifts to give the children. She had lived many years alone and needed little. She loved the children. She often smiled and had tears in her eyes when she saw a

small child. She thought of that baby she once had on the island off the coast. It was dead. She had no child of her own, but she had done all she could to save it.

After a few weeks she became weak. She loved to sit on the porch with the children. She loved to sing to them in her own words. She loved to attend the church. She had been given a name by the padre. No one knew her Indian name. She was called Juana Maria. Mrs. Nidiver tried to get her to eat her native foods. Juana Maria became very ill and died. She was buried at the Santa Barbara Mission.

Juana Maria never went to school. She spent all but a few weeks of her life on Ghalas-hat (San Nicolas Island). She spent 18 years of her life away from all people. She had seen the cruelty of people in the way they killed the sea otters and seals and even her own friends. She had lost all of her people. She was the last of the people of Ghalas-hat. She had learned her lessons of life very well. She knew how to care for her needs. She kept the fire burning. It never went out. She passed her tests and today her life teaches all of us what the commitment and the love of a mother for her child should mean.

This marker was placed on the wall of the Santa Barbara Mission near where the Lone Woman of Ghalas-hat was buried. They called her Juana Maria.